Ed retu

down and turned it on.

The envelopes started shooting in again. Ed's fingers punched the keyboard. The numbers flashed on the digital display.

13207 . . . 13090 . . . 08619 . . . KILL . . . 49548 . . .

Ed's mouth dropped open even as his fingers kept automatically punching.

21227 . . . 10977 . . . KILL'EM . . . 43310 . . .

Ed's gaze froze on the display. The big, busy room around him faded away. All he could see was the brightly-lit message.

KILL'EM ALL.

Ed Funsch was no longer bored to death.

He was scared to death.

Other X-Files books

#1 X Marks the Spot
#2 Darkness Falls
#3 Tiger, Tiger
#4 Squeeze
#5 Humbug
#6 Shapes

Voyager

THE X FILES™

FEAR

A novel by Les Martin

Based on the television series
The X-Files created by
Chris Carter

Based on the toleplay
written by Glen Morgan and
James Wong

HarperCollins*Publishers*

Voyager
An Imprint of HarperCollins*Publishers*
77–85 Fulham Palace Road,
Hammersmith, London W6 8JB

This paperback edition 1997
1 2 3 4 5 6 7 8 9

First published in the USA by HarperTrophy
A division of HarperCollins*Publishers* 1996

Cover photo by Michael Grecco

ISBN 0 583 33487 3

Set in Century

Printed in Great Britain by
Caledonian International Book Manufacturing Ltd, Glasgow

To Aaron,
the constant reader

FEAR

Chapter ONE

Ed Funsch was bored to death. His job did that to him sometimes. Most times, in fact. But then he reminded himself that it was better than starving to death. Or sleeping in the streets. Which was what he would have been doing if he hadn't landed this job two months ago.

Ed was working for the Postal Service in Franklin, Pennsylvania. Seven hours a day, five days a week, he sat in front of a mail sorting machine in the Postal Center.

Today was a working day like all the others. An envelope whisked into the sorter. Ed looked into a slotlike window. In it the zip code was highlighted.

14141

Ed tapped out the numbers on a numeric keyboard.

A red digital display on the machine lit up.

14141

Ed checked the number, then punched a button.

The letter zipped off to its next stop on the delivery chain.

Another letter whisked in to replace it.

02828

Ed tapped out the numbers.

02828

As the envelope zipped away, Ed glanced at his watch.

An hour and twenty minutes to lunch.

Then he looked back to see the next envelope arriving.

Ed had been working here a month now, one of many men in gray-and-blue uniforms at the Postal Center. By now he could do his work without thinking. He was free to think about other things.

One thing he thought more and more often was how much he hated the machine in front of him. It was the latest generation of sorting machines. It was supposed to be a great new tool for the working man.

What a laugh, Ed thought as he glared at the digital display. It was easy to see who was the tool. He wasn't running the machine. The machine was running him.

Suddenly he was jerked out of his thoughts.

The next envelope had jammed in the sorter.

Ed had to be grateful to envelopes like that. Funny-sized ones or ones with folds or wrinkles. They gave him something to do. Something that the machine couldn't. Not yet, anyway.

He reached in to free the envelope.

"Ouch!" he said, pulling his hand back.

He looked at his stinging finger. Blood was seeping out of it.

"A paper cut," he muttered, his stomach turning over.

The sight of blood made him feel sick, weaker than ever, more helpless than ever. He could practically feel the machine sneering at him. What chance did flesh and blood have against it? He started trembling with rage. He was seeing red, bloodred.

Just then a hand fell on Ed's shoulder.

Ed looked up. It was his supervisor, Harry McNally.

"Ed, you okay?" Harry asked, concerned. "You look pale as a ghost."

"Blood," said Ed, holding up his finger, still shaky.

Harry gave it a quick glance. "Just a paper cut, Ed." He paused, then said, "Still, if it really bothers you—"

"No, no," Ed said hastily. "You're right. It's nothing. Just about stopped bleeding already. I'll get right back to work. Gotta keep up with the job."

Harry cleared his throat. He looked uncomfortable.

"Ed," he said. "About that, the job I mean, I have to talk to you. Let's go over to the water cooler, where we can be by ourselves."

"But the letters," Ed said with a sinking feeling.

"Don't worry about them right now," Harry said. He reached around Ed and turned off the sorting machine.

Shoulders slumped, Ed stood up and followed Harry to the water cooler. He could guess what was coming. He had been through it before.

"Look, Ed, this is never easy," Harry said. "Everybody here likes you a lot. And I know it's tough because you're new in town. But, Ed, I'm sorry, I'm gonna have to let you go."

Ed didn't argue. He knew it would be useless. He just stood there, looking like a dog that had been whipped. A dog that hadn't done anything wrong. A dog looking at his master with accusing eyes.

Harry swallowed hard and explained, "It's not your work. Your work has been first-rate. And like I said, you're a good guy. But you know the story. There have been cutbacks. Downsizing. Budget problems—especially with the cost of new technology. And of course, with the new machines, we don't need as many—"

"Yeah, I know," Ed said. "It was like that with the last job I had. They got a machine that could do my work twice as fast and good as me. They told me it wasn't my fault. It was just progress."

"Of course, they need people to make those machines," said Harry. "Maybe you can get a training course and—"

"Harry, I'm fifty-two years old," Ed said. "Think I can learn new tricks? And if I did, would anybody hire someone my age on a starter's level?"

Harry didn't say anything.

"Look, Harry," Ed said. "Could I maybe work part-time?"

Harry sighed. "Don't think I wouldn't let you. But I got my orders. I'll show you the fax if you want."

"Nah, I believe you," said Ed.

Harry reached into his pocket and pulled out an envelope. "The guys took up a collection for you. It's a hundred bucks."

Awkwardly he stuffed the envelope into Ed's shirt pocket. Then he said, "Why don't you stay on till the end of the week. Sorry, but that's the best I can do."

"Don't apologize," said Ed. "Not your fault. Not anybody's fault. That's the trouble. Everybody's got their orders—right out of some machine or other."

Harry coughed. He gave Ed a quick pat on the back and went off. Ed returned to the sorting machine. He sat down and turned it on.

The envelopes started shooting in again. Ed's fingers punched the keyboard. The numbers flashed on the digital display.

13207 . . . 13090 . . . 08619 . . . KILL . . . 49548.

Ed's mouth dropped open even as his fingers kept automatically punching.

21227 . . . 10977 . . . KILL 'EM . . . 44310 . . .

Ed's gaze froze on the display. The big, busy room around him faded away. All he could see was the brightly lit message.

KILL 'EM ALL.

Ed Funsch was no longer bored to death.

He was scared to death.

Chapter TWO

Gary Taber had no worries about getting sacked from his job. He was his own boss, selling real estate. The trouble was, business was bad. Folks weren't buying houses or farms. Money was scarce in town—and in his bank account. He barely had enough to pay the landlord. Office rent was steep on the top floor of the Commercial Trust Building. It was Franklin's version of a skyscraper, a full ten stories high.

Gary looked at his watch. Time for lunch. The whole morning had gone by without a sale. Or even a nibble. It made a man angry, seeing so many years of building up a business go down the drain. Pretty soon he'd have to start brown-bagging lunch. Or skipping it.

Not today, though. His stomach was rumbling. He buttoned the collar of his white shirt, adjusted the knot on his tie, put on his gray suit jacket, and turned on his answering machine. His mouth was watering as he headed for the elevator. Corned beef and cabbage was the special of the day at Mulloy's café down the street.

The elevator was empty when he got in, but not for long. The green digital display inside changed from 10 to 9 and Gary had to move to the back as people poured in. Above the heads of the crowd, he saw 8 flash on. More passengers came aboard, the usual lunchtime crush. The trip down seemed to take forever, with stops at every floor. Gary truly hated this elevator ride. Closed, crowded spaces drove him crazy. Maybe losing his office wouldn't be so bad. He'd be out on the street, but he'd never have to be stuck in this elevator again.

Gary looked at the digital display to see how many floors were left before he could get out of there.

It read: NO AIR.

Sweat poured down Gary's face. He mopped his forehead with the back of his hand. His lungs ached. All these people, hemming him in. If only they would go away.

CAN'T BREATHE, flashed the digital display.

Gary's hand clawed at his tie to loosen it. He backed away from the digital display, but his back hit the wall. There was nowhere to go.

The people near him edged away from him, pressing toward the front. But they had nowhere to go, either. They could only watch the digital display and see it flash 3, then 2.

They all shared a single unsaid thought. *Thank goodness this ride will soon be over*. In another minute the sweating, weaving, gasping, bug-eyed man in the back might be sick all over them. Or he might totally collapse. Whatever happened, they'd be late to lunch.

None of them could see what Gary Taber saw as he stared at the digital display.

If they had, they would have worried about more than lunch.

Gary's eyes seemed to bulge out of his head as he read:

KILL 'EM ALL!

"Four dead—not counting the killer," said Jim Spencer. He was a tall, powerfully built man with a neatly trimmed mustache and a sharply pressed uniform. He was the sheriff commander of Venango County, Pennsylvania, and he looked the part.

The man with him wore a slightly rumpled suit and could have used a haircut. He didn't look like what Spencer had expected to get when the sheriff asked the FBI Behavioral Science Unit for help.

Even the agent's name was off the wall. Who ever heard of a G-man with the first name Fox?

Still, Spencer was making the best of it. He had to. He needed someone to make sense out of a case that was driving him crazy. As he told Mulder, "I'm relieved the bureau answered our request. Because in all honesty, whatever's going on is way over our heads."

"I expect that's why they sent me," Mulder told him. "Unusual cases are my specialty."

"I know that you people usually profile suspects still at large," said Spencer. "It must seem odd being asked to profile suspects who are all dead."

"As I said, 'odd' is par for the course," Mulder said.

The two men stood in the lobby of the Commercial Trust Building. In front of them a yellow ribbon was stretched chest high. On it bold black print declared, CRIME SCENE: DO NOT CROSS.

A deputy lifted the ribbon for them to duck under. They went to the elevator that stood with its door open. One body lay under a tarp halfway out the door. The other three bodies lay under tarps inside the elevator.

Mulder was all business. Swiftly he slid on latex gloves so as not to contaminate the crime scene. He moved into the elevator, with Spencer close behind.

As Mulder examined the corpses, Spencer continued to fill him in. "The suspect's body is out on the sidewalk. We're holding the security guard who shot him. Surviving witnesses from the elevator are down at the hospital. You can talk to them whenever you're ready."

Mulder nodded, only half listening. Spencer watched him, his professional curiosity mixing with something close to awe. The sheriff had never seen an investigator work so fast. This was big-league stuff. A small-town lawman had a lot to learn from it.

After Mulder finished with the corpses, he turned to examine the elevator. He looked at the waist-high railing, the call buttons, the ceiling.

"We sketched the area, and we're set to dust for prints," Spencer said. He wanted the FBI man to know that, locals or not, they weren't total amateurs.

"Did that damage occur during the incident?" asked Mulder. He pointed to the digital display. It was bashed in.

Spencer hadn't noticed the wreckage. His face flushed. He swallowed and said, "I'll find out."

Mulder nodded. "May I see the suspect?"

"You can see what's left of him," said the sheriff.

Chapter THREE

"Things like this aren't supposed to happen here," said the sheriff as he and Mulder left the Commercial Trust Building.

"A forty-two-year-old real estate agent murders four strangers?" said Mulder. "That's not supposed to happen anywhere."

"Of course, of course," Spencer said. "But what I mean is, there's only been three murders in these parts since colonial times. That is, before this craziness started. In the last six months, seven people have killed twenty-two. In terms of population, you have any idea how high a homicide rate that is?"

"High," said Mulder. "Definitely high."

"It's higher than the combined homicide rates of Detroit, Washington, D.C., and Los Angeles," said Spencer. "Combined."

He grabbed Mulder by the arm. "Franklin is not remotely like any of those cities," Spencer said. "We're simple, ordinary folk around here, all getting along together. There's no glitz and no ghettos. No riots and no muggings."

Mulder nodded. "Point taken," he said.

Satisfied, Spencer led him outside. Halfway down the block a body lay under a tarp. There was dried blood around the covering. Uniformed police officers were keeping onlookers away. The cops and civilians shared the same stunned look.

"After each outbreak of violence, the suspect was killed?" Mulder asked Spencer.

"Suicide by cop," Spencer said.

"Which means?" asked Mulder.

"Each killing spree occurred in a public place," Spencer explained. "The suspect went berserk and would not stop when ordered. Officers on the scene had to use deadly force to save lives."

"Were the suspects checked for substance abuse?"

"Agent Mulder," Spencer said, "this town is made up mostly of apple and cherry growers. These folks don't even drink much. They certainly don't do drugs."

"Were they checked?" Mulder persisted.

"Yes," Spencer said. "The coroner's tests were negative."

Mulder squatted, lifted the tarp, and began looking over the bullet-ridden body of Gary Taber.

The sheriff forced himself not to turn his eyes away. But his face went pale.

"I played softball with this guy over Labor Day," he said. "He was one of those real nice guys. The kind that can't really play and doesn't complain about being stuck in right field—"

Lost in memory, Spencer added, "He was always the first one to shake hands at the end of a game."

Mulder lifted the corpse's hand for a closer look. It was stiff with rigor mortis, but he was able to turn it palm up. Under the nail of the index finger was a greenish yellow substance. Whatever it was, it was not dirt.

"He bought a round of Cokes for us afterward," Spencer recalled. He looked off into space as Mulder pulled a plastic evidence bag over Taber's hand and secured it.

"Have the substance under the fingernail analyzed by the bureau lab," Mulder said, rising.

"Right," Spencer said. "I'll get right on it."

To himself he said, "What on earth could bring anyone to do this?"

In a bank lobby across town, Ed Funsch was looking at his cut finger and wondering much the same thing.

Under the Band-Aid the finger still ached. So did the memory of the murderous message on the mail sorter's digital display.

It was as if the machine had smelled blood and gone after him. It was as if it knew how the sight of blood awakened old fear in him, and how weak it made him feel.

He had fooled it, though. He hated it too much to let it tell him what to do. Machines had wrecked his life, taking one job after another. As far as Ed was concerned, they should take all the machines on earth and send them into outer space.

He sighed. Trouble was, you couldn't escape them anymore. Today he had left the Postal Center for good. He had told the supervisor to forget about his working out the week. But then he had to go straight to another machine, an ATM. He wanted to deposit the money the guys had given him, so that he wouldn't be tempted to spend it too fast. And he had to use an ATM—the bank charged extra if you used a live teller.

The man in front of Ed at the ATM finished with it, and Ed took his place.

PLEASE INSERT YOUR CARD the digital display commanded, and Ed obeyed.

DEPOSIT? WITHDRAWAL? ACCOUNT BALANCE? the display asked.

Ed was about to punch in the answer when he heard a woman's voice say, "You're bleeding!"

Sweat broke out on Ed's face. He whirled around.

A mother was bending over her little daughter, applying a tissue to the girl's nose.

"I told you not to pick at it," the woman scolded.

Ed barely heard her. He stared at the spots of red on the tissue. They made him sweat even more. His stomach turned over.

Getting a grip on himself, he turned back to the machine and stared at the display.

SECURITY GUARD he read. The words flashed like a pounding heart.

Automatically Ed looked at the security guard who stood outside the bank door.

Then he turned back to the display.

TAKE HIS GUN it told him.

Ed could not stop himself from looking back at the guard—and at the holstered gun on his belt.

Ed shut his eyes hard.

But he couldn't keep them shut.

It was as if fingers were pulling his eyelids open to read the next message on the machine.

KILL 'EM ALL

Ed did the only thing he could do.

He hit the Cancel button on the machine with his fist.

Again and again and again.

The security guard saw him and came running.

"Hey, what do you think you're doing?" he demanded.

Ed kept punching.

"What's wrong with you, mister?" the guard demanded, grabbing Ed's arm.

Ed shook him off.

Then Ed was off and running.

He had to get away from the machine. He had to get away from the guard.

But how could he get away from himself?

Chapter FOUR

Mulder sat alone late at night in the sheriff's office.

But he didn't feel alone.

With him were the corpses from the Commercial Trust Building elevator—that is, police photos of them, tacked to a large bulletin board. With him, too, were photos of the victims of the other recent killings.

Tacked up beside them were snapshots of the killers, taken long before the crimes. Mulder had been looking at them all again and again, for hours now. But so far they had told him nothing.

Mulder was with someone else as well.

The modem on his laptop computer connected him with Scully. He could imagine her face as he tapped out his report, as it appeared on her monitor.

In his mind's eye, Mulder saw Scully sitting in front of the computer terminal in her office at FBI Headquarters in Washington, D.C. She would be wearing her glasses as she looked at the brightly lit screen. They always made her look a little bit like a schoolteacher. A very pretty, well-groomed schoolteacher, to be sure. But one who still graded a report for errors in fact and flaws in logic. Especially if the report came from her partner, Fox Mulder.

It went against Scully's grain to accept many of Mulder's far-out ideas. She liked her explanations down-to-earth.

For once, Mulder hoped she came up with a nice, levelheaded explanation. This case had him stumped.

"People who commit murder are divided into two general types," he tapped out. "There are spree killers, who go on a deadly rampage because of a sudden explosion of insane anger. And there are serial killers, who kill again and again over a long period of time because of a deep-rooted mental disorder."

Mulder paused and looked again at the photos of the dead killers. They were far different from the grainy black-and-white pictures of the slain victims in their blood-soaked clothing. The photos of the killers were cheerful color snapshots of smiling men and women.

Mulder sighed and went back to typing his report. "The killers do not fit the profiles of either spree killers or serial killers. Indeed, they would seem more likely to be such killers' victims instead."

Mulder gave the snapshots another look and

continued typing. A frown line formed between his eyebrows. "The killers were all middle-income, responsible people. None had a history of any kind of serious mental disorder. None had a history of any kind of violence. Relatives and friends report only minor signs of disturbance. Slight sleep disorders. Headaches. Lack of appetite and binge eating. But nothing that can be considered more than a normal part of the stress of ordinary life."

Mulder paused and examined the snapshot of Gary Taber. Gary was standing next to a barbecue grill. He was proudly holding up a hot dog he had finished grilling on the end of a long fork. In his free hand he held a bun. A young, freckle-faced blond boy, his son, stood grinning beside him.

This was a man who had savagely slain four people?

Mulder shook his head and went back to his typing. "Survivors of the latest killings report that the suspect did show signs of acute discomfort in the elevator. But none of this seems nearly enough to explain the extreme violence of the crime." Mulder paused again.

Mulder had a face that looked quite young, younger than he was. But there were times when he looked quite old.

Tonight, as he tried to think what else he could tell

Scully about this case, Mulder looked very old indeed.

As he stared into space, his hands poised over the computer keys, he stiffened. In the distance he heard a low rumbling like thunder. His brow furrowed. The night was cloudless. There wasn't a hint of a storm anywhere.

Then, as quickly as it had come, the rumbling went away, and Mulder started typing again.

Dana Scully sat in her office watching her computer screen waiting for Mulder to continue.

Minutes ticked by.

Just as she began to think the modem had been left hanging, fresh words appeared on her screen.

"I am convinced that an outside factor must be responsible. But I must admit I have no idea what it can be."

Scully's eyes filled with concern. It was not like Mulder to sound so discouraged.

She felt herself growing tense as she waited for him to go on.

Mulder looked at a photo of Gary Taber's hand. He flipped the pages of the lab report on the substance under Taber's fingernail. Maybe Scully could spot something he couldn't, he thought, as he hunched over his laptop again.

"A residue discovered under the fingernail of the most recent suspect was analyzed," he typed. "It turns out to be an undefined but nontoxic chemical found on plants. Most probably it is the remains of gardening activity, quite normal in this agricultural community."

Scully's finger tapped impatiently on her desktop as Mulder came to a stop again.

Finally new words began to appear.

"There have been reported cases of mental disorder caused by UFO abductions. Several people who claim to have been abducted have displayed extreme paranoia, quite possibly justified."

Scully smiled.

"I was wondering when you'd get to that, partner," she said under her breath, as she waited for Mulder to go on.

Her smile faded as she read, "I find no evidence, however, that this or any other UFO phenomenon applies to this case. None at all."

There was another pause.

More words appeared, more slowly than before. Scully could see how weary Mulder was getting.

"The various killings seem to be connected by only one common thread. In each case, an electronic device at the crime scene was destroyed. There was a pager. A fax machine. A cellular phone. An elevator digital display. And so on. But . . ."

Another pause.

Then: "But none of this seems to tell me anything. In all honesty, Scully, I've never had a more difficult time developing a theory of what is behind a crime."

The next pause lasted only a few seconds.

"There is no way to know who will be a killer. Or who will be killed."

Scully stared at Mulder's sign-off. She tried to think of an argument that would convince her superiors to send her to the scene. She was sure Mulder needed her help more than he ever had.

His last words lingered on the screen. Scully felt a chill as she reread them.

"There is no way to know who will be a killer. Or who will be killed."

Chapter FIVE

Mrs. Bonnie McRoberts loved her husband, Sam. But sometimes she wished he weren't always so busy at his job. She wished he were around more when she needed him. Like now.

Bonnie was standing on a street corner on the edge of Franklin. The neighborhood was the closest thing the town had to a slum. Bonnie had come there straight from work and felt out of place in her smartly tailored business suit. She could feel the people on the run-down street staring at her in the gathering dark. Yet she hesitated before going into the grimy garage on the corner.

Her husband had said she'd save a lot of money by taking their car here to be fixed. He'd heard that Ace Auto Repairs did good work cheap. But he wasn't the one who had to bring it in or pick it up. That was her job, as far as he was concerned, since she was the one who'd had the accident. Not that it had been such a big thing. Just a little flash of anger when the guy in the Camaro cut in front of her, radio blaring. Sam, though, wouldn't believe it wasn't all her fault. He said she was just too nervous behind the wheel. Worst of all, she knew people would agree with him. She might be a well-dressed, well-paid legal secretary downtown, but in the eyes of the men around here, she was just another terrible woman driver.

Take the man who ran this shop. Talk about macho. A real male chauvinist pig. He hadn't even tried to hide his sneer when he saw the damage and she tried to explain it. And she could see the greedy gleam in his eyes as he figured out how much he could charge her for the repairs. She would have asked her husband to help, but her pride wouldn't let her. That would have made Sam surer than ever that she was just some weak, defenseless woman.

The trouble was, she had to admit, she did feel pretty defenseless right now. She was at this miserable mechanic's mercy. How could she make sure he didn't sense how lost she felt when he talked about carburetors and batteries and gearboxes and transmissions and brake linings and all the other junk under the hood? How could she keep him from coming after her credit card like a shark scenting blood?

Bonnie straightened her spine, smoothed her skirt, and strode into the garage.

Her nose wrinkled at the stench of oil and grease and lord knew what else. The place was dark except for the glow of a mechanic's hood lamp at the far end of the cavelike room. The light was coming from under the raised hood of her Volvo.

"Hello," Bonnie called out as she approached it.

The mechanic came out from under the hood. His name was Joey.

He wiped his greasy hands on his even greasier coveralls as he recognized Bonnie.

"You're late," he told her. "Time is money, y'know."

"I'm sorry," Bonnie said. "I called to say I was delayed. But nobody answered. And your machine wasn't on."

"Ain't got no machine," Joey said. "I run a bare-bones operation. That's how I charge as low as I do."

"There was a crisis in the office. A last-minute job. As I said, I'm sorry."

Bonnie stopped herself there. She reminded herself not to show this guy any hint of weakness or fear. "If the car's ready," she said, "I'll just have a look at your bill, pay up, and drive away."

"You really did a number on this baby," Joey said, scratching his shaggy head. A filthy red bandanna was tied around it. It made him look even more like a pirate than he was.

"Were you able to fix it?" asked Bonnie evenly.

"Sure, I can fix most anything."

"Fine," said Bonnie, hoping Joey could not sense her inward sigh of relief. "Then I'll take care of your bill and—"

"Trouble is," Joey said, "in fixing it, I found some other problems. Serious problems, Mrs. McRoberts."

Lights flashed in Bonnie's brain. Warning lights.

"Come here and I'll show you," Joey said, moving toward the front of the car.

When Bonnie was a little girl, her father used to scare her with stories of the boogeyman. As the mechanic motioned for her to come and stand by his side, she thought of the boogeyman, of her wild fear when she heard his name. . .

Come on, Bonnie, you're a big girl now, she told herself, keeping her face impassive and her step confident as she joined Joey.

She had barely reached the mechanic when the car's engine roared into life. She almost jumped out of her skin.

"Sorry if I scared you, Mrs. McRoberts," said Joey, not sounding sorry at all. "Or maybe you'd like me to call you Bonnie."

"Ms. McRoberts will do fine," Bonnie said. "So will an explanation of what you're doing."

"See this here machine," Joey said, giving her a look at the apparatus hooked up to her car motor. "It's an engine analyzer. You press this button and the engine starts. The machine checks out how the different parts are working. And you can read the results in this here monitor."

Joey pressed a button and the engine roared again.

"See, you're supposed to have an output of a hundred and sixty-eight horses at sixty-two hundred RPMs," Joey said. "You're nowhere near that."

"Yes, I see," said Bonnie. As far as she was concerned, Joey might have been talking Greek.

Joey's grin grew wider.

"That's just for starters," he said. "Take a look at this."

He revved the motor again and made room for Bonnie to read the monitor.

Bonnie told herself to look as intelligent as she could, though she had no hope of deciphering what it said.

She was wrong.

The message on the monitor was clear.

LIAR

Dimly she heard Joey's voice droning on behind her.

"The ignition firing order is out of whack. Plus the transmission is shot. Not to mention . . ."

Bonnie paid no attention. Her eyes were glued to the monitor.

HE'S A LIAR it told her.

"Fixing it will cost you, but I'll give you a good deal because you're such a nice lady," Joey went on.

Sweat beaded Bonnie's forehead as she read, HE'S RIPPING YOU OFF BECAUSE YOU'RE A WOMAN.

"If you don't do it, you can just put your car on the junk heap," Joey said.

HE WANTS TO DESTROY YOUR CAR. HE WANTS TO DESTROY YOU. DESTROY HIM INSTEAD, the monitor commanded. KILL HIM!

"Like I said, Bonnie, I mean, Mrs. McRoberts, the choice is yours," Joey said.

KILL HIM NOW! The monitor's message seared into Bonnie's brain like lightning.

Screaming with rage she scooped up a wrench from the greasy concrete floor.

"Hey . . . wha—?" was all Joey got out before the wrench smashed him across the forehead.

With the back of one grimy hand the mechanic wiped away the blood pouring from his forehead. With the other hand, he grabbed a hammer.

At the same time, his foot came up.

The vicious kick caught Bonnie in the kneecap. She fell backward, crashing into a workbench and dropping the wrench.

"I'll get you, you little—" Joey snarled as he came toward her, hammer raised high.

Bonnie looked for something, anything, to use as

a weapon against him. Then she saw it—the hard, sharp, triangular end of an oil can spout.

She clutched at the spout as Joey lifted the hammer higher, preparing to strike.

She stepped aside as he swung.

At the same time she drove the metal spout deep into his chest.

His body hit the concrete floor and lay still.

Bonnie's high heels splashed briskly through the blood and oil as she walked to her car engine, detached the machine from it, and lowered the hood.

She took one last look at the monitor.

It read: ANALYSIS COMPLETE. NEXT.

Bonnie opened her car door, got behind the wheel, and turned on the ignition.

As she had expected, the motor sounded just fine.

Chapter SIX

"I don't know why you bothered coming along, Agent Mulder," Spencer said. "This murder clearly has nothing to do with your investigation."

"I'm sorry if I seem to be intruding on your turf, Sheriff," said Mulder. "I certainly don't question your competence. But part of my investigation is to see if this death is connected."

"Have it your way," Spencer said with a shrug. "You do your job. I'll do mine. We'll see who comes up with the killer first."

They stood in the gloom of the Ace Auto Repairs garage. It was morning, but the early daylight barely filtered through the small, dirt-crusted windows. Police floodlights illuminated the scene of the crime.

The mechanic's body had been taken to the morgue for an autopsy. But there was no mystery about how he had died. The puncture wound in his chest and the oil spout with the bloody tip told the story.

Mulder looked at a photo of the corpse, then at the bloody wrench in its plastic evidence bag. He glanced around the garage at the police dusting the place for fingerprints, collecting samples of spilled blood, making measurements of every kind, and otherwise looking as busy as they could.

A shadow of a smile crossed Mulder's face. He suspected that the local law was going all out to put on a good show for the outsider from the FBI.

Too bad they were getting nowhere.

"We'll identify the killer within hours," Sheriff Spencer said. "The wrench and the oil spout were loaded with fingerprints. As soon as we run them through the state police and FBI computer files, we'll have our man."

"Presuming the killer was a man," said Mulder.

"Considering the violence of the crime, I think that goes without saying," said Spencer.

"And also presuming the prints are on file," Mulder went on. "Presuming the killer was not a law-abiding citizen who had no fingerprint record. Presuming the killer was not like the other killers in this case."

Spencer began in a slightly annoyed voice, "As I've already indicated, I think it is quite clear that—"

He was interrupted by a new arrival, a tall, well-dressed, well-groomed man in his forties. Everything about him spoke of authority.

"Hi, Spence, how's it coming along?" he asked.

"As well as can be expected, Larry." When the newcomer gave Mulder a curious glance, Spencer added, "Larry, this is FBI Agent Mulder. He's here on special assignment at our request. Agent Mulder, this is Larry Winter, county supervisor."

Larry Winter put out his hand for a handshake.

"Do you know," he asked Mulder, "is this murder more of the same?"

Before Mulder could answer, Spencer cut in. "They don't seem to be connected," he said.

Winter turned to the sheriff. "Should I be relieved—or scared? Is this the start of an epidemic of copycat killings?"

"I believe we can safely say this was not a copy of the other homicides," Spencer said. "The murder was not committed in a public area. The suspect fled, covering his tracks. The killer appears not to have had a premeditated weapon. All this adds up to an ordinary crime of violence rather than the craziness we've been experiencing."

"Is that your opinion as well, Agent Mulder?" asked the county supervisor.

"It's too early in the investigation to have firm opinions," Mulder said. "I'm merely gathering as many pieces of information as I can. Hopefully, at some point they'll fit together to reveal a pattern in these seemingly random crimes. A pattern that right now remains hidden."

Winter nodded. "Like fitting together pieces of a jigsaw puzzle to get a picture?"

"That's one way of putting it," Mulder said. "But in this case, the pieces are more oddly shaped than usual. They're harder to fit together to form any picture that we can recognize."

Sheriff Spencer shook his head. "When it comes to this garage murder, I don't agree. We have practically everything we need to crack the case. The only big hole in the evidence is a motive. And to find that, I say we follow the golden rule of tracking down a criminal. We follow the money. Let me show you what I've dug up already."

The sheriff started to lead them toward his discovery, but Mulder stopped him.

"Let me check out one more thing," he said.

Mulder had spotted a machine with a large digital display monitor at the back of the garage. Now he headed for it like a bee going after honey.

When he reached the machine, he saw that the digital display was intact. He read its message: ANALYSIS COMPLETE. NEXT.

"Convinced now?" said the sheriff. "You can cross this off your list of crimes to worry about."

"I can't argue," Mulder conceded. He gave the flashing digital display one last glance and then followed Spencer and Winter through a peeling wooden door into a tiny office. A battered oak desk was littered with piles of bills and invoices.

"I've already been through some of them," Spencer said. "I can tell you one reason somebody might have killed the mechanic. This guy was a thief. Take a look at the parts he billed for, and compare them with the parts he actually ordered. This shop had to be the rip-off capital of the auto world. That explains why there isn't a single car to be repaired here. People must have started getting wise."

Mulder was only half listening as he flipped through the papers on the desk.

Spencer was right. It was easy to see what a crook the mechanic had been. There were invoices for minor parts like oil filters and air filters. With them were bills to customers for complete transmission systems and other major jobs.

Suddenly Mulder froze.

He took another look at the invoice he had just read. Then he read it one more time.

"MAKE OF AUTO: 1991 Volvo sedan. Owner: Mrs. Bonnie McRoberts, 50 Oak Lane. PARTS SUPPLIED: Digital Dashboard Clock/Mileage Readout. Part #149WX541. SERVICE: Replace smashed readout in dashboard."

His mouth formed a silent whistle. Then he said urgently, "The crime *is* connected. Come on! We've got to move fast."

Chapter SEVEN

Bonnie McRoberts was just putting the finishing touches on her makeup when the doorbell rang.

"Drat," she said to herself. Someone at the door, just when she was in a hurry. She had forgotten to set the alarm clock. She was way behind schedule—and being late to work was the last thing she wanted. The law firm she worked for had merged with another a year ago. Since then the staff had been steadily reduced. Nobody knew who would be next. And if Bonnie was laid off, gone would be her health insurance, the next mortgage payment on the house, and maybe even her marriage. She didn't know how she and Sam would get along if they had to scrimp on every little thing that made life nice, and it scared her to think of it.

Thoroughly annoyed, she opened the door.

She saw a youngish-looking man in a dark suit. Behind him was a neatly mustached man in a county police uniform.

Mulder saw a woman as neat, trim, and proper as her white-shuttered, green-lawned home. She was dressed in a smartly cut gray suit.

"Mrs. Bonnie McRoberts?" he asked.

"Yes."

"I'm Special Agent Fox Mulder. Federal Bureau of Investigation," said Mulder, showing her his bureau ID. "This is Sheriff Spencer. We'd like to ask you a few questions."

"Look, I'd like to help you gentlemen," said Bonnie. "But I'm late for work. Perhaps at lunchtime—"

"I'm sorry, but this is urgent," Mulder said. "If you're late, you can blame me. May we come in?"

Bonnie shrugged and opened the door wider. After Mulder and Spencer entered, she closed the door and led them through the living room toward the kitchen.

"I'm sorry the house is such a mess," she said, though Mulder could see nothing out of order. "It's so hard, holding down a job and keeping the place neat. My husband is okay about doing the lawn and raking leaves and all that. But he acts like using a vacuum cleaner and a dust cloth is against the law for a man. Not to mention a washing machine, a dishwasher, and a microwave. Speaking of which, is it all right if I make myself some breakfast?"

"It's the day's most important meal," Mulder said.

"I wish I had time to have a better one," said

Bonnie. "But it's busy, busy, busy. Sometimes I get so tired I could scream."

"A woman's work is never done," agreed Mulder.

"Can I offer you gentlemen something?" Bonnie asked, taking a package of English muffins out of the freezer.

"No, thank you. We breakfasted early," Mulder said.

"Doughnuts, I bet," Bonnie said. "I've heard that's what policemen feed on."

"Day and night, unfortunately," said Spencer, whose stomach bulged over his wide leather belt. "Got to cut down, I keep telling myself."

He gave Mulder a glance, silently asking why on earth they were bothering this very nice woman.

"Been having some car trouble?" Mulder asked Bonnie as she put a muffin into the microwave.

"That's my husband's department," said Bonnie, punching a button. The microwave display flashed on: DEFROST.

"May I speak to him?"

"He just took the car to Pittsburgh for a business meeting. Left at dawn. Poor guy, works almost as hard as I do," said Bonnie, waiting for the display to tell her when the muffin was done.

Instead it told her something else.

HE KNOWS flashed on the display.

At the same time, Mulder pulled a piece of paper from his pocket. "This auto repair work order has your name on it. And it was signed by you. Did you by any chance pick up your car last night?" he asked.

The microwave beeped.

Bonnie's eyes went back to the display.

KILL 'EM BOTH! it read.

"Yes," she said.

"And when you picked it up, did you happen to notice . . . ?" Mulder began to ask. Then he realized Bonnie wasn't looking at him. She was staring at the microwave display.

He looked at the display. It was giving a clock reading: 7:35 A.M.

From the panicked look on Bonnie's face, she had to be really worried about being late to work. She didn't seem to have heard a word he'd said.

As she took the muffin out of the microwave, he tried again. "Mrs. McRoberts, can you describe how the dashboard readout on your car became damaged?"

Behind Mulder, Spencer scratched his head. What dashboard readout was Mulder talking about?

Bonnie looked just as puzzled. She shook her head dully as she sliced open the muffin and spread it with strawberry jam.

"Mrs. McRoberts," Mulder said insistently. "I think you owe me an answer."

He tried to look her in the eye, but Bonnie turned her head away. She stared out the window, trembling, as if that were the only safe place in the world she could look.

"Who did it?" Mulder asked gently. "How did it happen?"

Her whole body shaking, Bonnie answered, "I did it. I broke it. Please, don't ask any more."

"Why? Why did you do it?" Mulder went on. "Did you see something in the readout?"

Eyes closed, Bonnie shook her head. But she couldn't keep back a sob.

"I can help," Mulder said. "Tell me what you saw."

Gently he touched her shoulder.

It was enough to make her eyes fly open.

But still she did not look at Mulder. Instead her eyes went to the microwave display.

Mulder's eyes followed hers.

All he saw was the time.

He would never know what she saw.

Then there was the flash of a metal blade as Bonnie grabbed a kitchen knife from the countertop.

Mulder raised his arm to fend off the blade as it slashed toward his chest.

Pain cut across his forearm as he leaped backward. Blood reddened his sleeve.

Behind him he heard Spencer shouting, "Stop!"

Bonnie had hit Mulder with the full force of her body as he retreated. Caught off balance, he went down on his back. Instantly she was on him.

Mulder looked into her eyes as she raised the knife again.

It was like looking into a night without moon or stars. It was like looking into his own grave.

The gunshot, when he heard it, sounded almost distant to him—though it was deafeningly loud and came from Sheriff Spencer's gun just a few feet away.

Chapter EIGHT

The corpse of Bonnie McRoberts had arrived at the FBI lab an hour ago.

In the lab, Scully put on an apron, goggles, and latex gloves.

Bonnie's death-pale body lay on a snow-white sheet. Aside from the damage caused by the four bullets that had ended her life, her body was in excellent shape.

Scully adjusted an overhead microphone and snapped on a tape recorder before she made her first incision.

She was all business as she began dissecting.

Her voice did not waver as she reported her findings.

Mulder could practically hear that calm voice as he read Scully's report on Bonnie McRoberts.

He sat in his hotel room, in front of his laptop, watching Scully's words appear:

"Several unusual features were discovered during this examination. They were not detected in autopsies of previous slain suspects, though it is possible they were there as well," Scully typed. "Levels of adrenaline are known to be high in cases of violent death, twice as much as in victims of natural death. But Bonnie McRoberts's adrenaline level was two hundred times normal."

Mulder's eyes widened. Adrenaline was powerful stuff. The body's adrenal gland produced it in moments of fear. Or anger. Or both. It was a reaction to danger. Or stress. Or both. In extreme cases, it could produce bursts of superhuman strength. People had been known to lift automobiles from the ground with their bare hands under its influence. It was hard to imagine what "two hundred times normal" could empower a person to do.

One thing Mulder could be sure of: that level was more than enough to give a man the strength and speed to kill four people in an elevator in a matter of minutes. It was also enough to make Mulder lucky to be alive, after his encounter with Bonnie McRoberts.

He patted his heavily bandaged arm and went back to Scully's report:

"The woman's adrenal gland displayed considerable damage. But not from disease. The damage appears to be caused by overuse—prolonged and unusual wear and tear. Evidence in other body parts indicates an extraordinary number of episodes of intense fear or rage or both."

Mulder's mind flashed back to when he had seen Bonnie McRoberts alive. She had been exceptionally upset about being late to work. He made a mental note to check up on her job situation, even as he watched Scully's words scroll onward:

"My final test was on a fluid taken from the subject's eyeball. I found a high concentration of an unknown chemical compound. This compound is markedly similar to the substance analyzed earlier on another suspect's finger."

So there is a connection between at least two of the killers, Gary Taber and Bonnie McRoberts, Mulder thought. He leaned toward the monitor. He did not want to miss a word of Scully's analysis of that connection.

"I will have to make further tests to be sure, but I will hazard a guess. It is my opinion that this unknown chemical can form a highly potent substance when it mixes with adrenaline and other compounds produced during periods of fear or anger. This substance is similar to, though probably not exactly like, lysergic acid diethylamide."

Mulder did not have to wait for Scully to explain what lysergic acid diethylamide was. He already knew what it was and what it could do. It could twist the human mind like a pretzel, turn it upside down and inside out, make it shoot off into space like a skyrocket and explode in a million colors.

Mulder's own mind was already whirling with possibilities as he stared at Scully's last word on the subject:

"LSD."

Chapter NINE

Ed Funsch wiped sweat from his brow. He felt scared. Not that that was unusual. It seemed like he was scared all the time now. More and more scared.

Funny thing, though, he had never been so angry, either. All that bad stuff piling up on him. Getting fired from that job in the Postal Service was the final straw. The job wasn't much, but at least it was supposed to be safe. Big laugh, with the joke on him. It was enough to make any man mad.

"Hey, Ed, get ahold of yourself," he said to himself. "You can't let folks see you so upset. Nobody's gonna hire a sore loser. Just like nobody's gonna believe those things you keep reading on those screens. They'd lock you in the nuthouse and throw away the key. You gotta tell yourself those crazy words were some kind of bad dream. You gotta wake up and shape up."

Nervously Ed glanced around at the people standing in the line with him. He was afraid his lips had been moving. They would think he was crazy. But he saw he could relax. Nobody was looking at him.

The line was moving fast. In a few minutes it was his turn at the counter.

A bored-looking man in shirtsleeves looked Ed up and down.

"Yeah?" he asked in a dead voice.

"I was just wondering if Superstores needed any help," Ed said. "I mean, I could do anything. Be a salesclerk. Make deliveries. Work in the stockroom. Or maybe be a night watchman. Or if you need someone, you know, to keep the place clean, mop up, polish glass, stuff like that. Any shift you need people. And it doesn't have to be here at this store. I mean, I know you're a big chain. I can go anyplace you have an opening."

Thc hiring clerk gave Ed another once-over. Ed knew what the man saw. He could see himself in the man's cold eyes. A fifty-two-year-old has-been in a cheap suit, a shirt with a frayed collar, a tie with food spots on it, and shoes with run-down heels.

Ed knew what the man would say before he said it.

"Sorry, we're not hiring. Maybe in a couple of months, if business picks up for Christmas."

Sure, Ed thought, *I believe that. Just like I believe in Santa Claus.*

"Well, thanks anyway," Ed forced himself to say. Shoulders slumped, he shuffled away from the counter. He headed toward the exit. He reminded himself to stop in the food department and pick up a can of beans for supper.

He never made it to the food department. He was stopped by a large sign that seemed to hit him between the eyes.

BLOOD it said in bright red letters.

The sign was pasted on a booth where two smiling middle-aged women sat.

The first one saw Ed stop dead in his tracks in front of the booth. "Sir, may we ask you to sign up for the town blood drive?" she asked in a bright, cheerful voice.

The second woman smiled brightly at Ed and held out a ballpoint pen.

The smiles on both women's faces faded when they saw Ed's reaction.

The word BLOOD swam before his eyes, as if the red letters were flowing like blood.

He staggered away from the booth, crashing into a woman with a baby in a carrier on her back.

"Sorry, ma'am, sorry," Ed muttered, blinking hard, hurrying away.

Then he was in the television section of the store. Twenty display sets were turned on, each showing a different program.

Ed looked desperately at the screens. Anything

to get that bright red word out of his mind! Besides, TV had always been a weakness of his, the only way he knew to get his mind off his troubles.

And now, for just a little while, it did.

He watched a cartoon cat chasing a cartoon mouse and chuckled. He watched a weatherman pointing at a satellite photo and started to relax. He watched a woman selling gold bracelets, a man talking over a moving stock market ticker, a patient on an operating table in a soap opera, and a pitcher delivering a sharp breaking curve.

Then, in front of Ed's widening eyes, the pictures changed.

He saw a man being brutally beaten by police. He saw a sniper on top of a building firing at innocent people below. He saw skinheads screaming out hate and a serial killer talking placidly about his victims. He saw a nightmare of video violence in America.

"No . . . no . . . no," he gasped. But he could not turn his eyes away, as new pictures flashed on faster and faster, brighter and bloodier.

His eyes sought escape on the single screen that had no picture.

It just had words: BEHIND YOU.

Ed turned around.

He saw hunting rifles. Racks and racks of them,

under glass. All for sale to anyone with a few dollars. Each guaranteed to give a big bang for the buck.

Blinking, Ed turned back to the TV.

Its message was short and sweet.

DO IT.

Chapter TEN

Mulder went to see the Lone Gunmen in Washington, D.C. Their names were Byers, Langly, and Frohike. From their Washington office they published a magazine, plugged into the Internet, and otherwise spread their words and views around the country and the world.

Mulder took a flight to D.C. from Franklin. As far as the FBI was concerned, Byers, Langly, and Frohike made even Mulder seem sane.

Mulder had to agree that Byers, Langly, and Frohike were unusual. But so were a lot of things that kept happening all over the world. Things that the bureau couldn't or wouldn't explain. And what Mulder needed explained now was crazy enough to be right down the Lone Gunmen's dark and twisted alley of sinister secrets and danger in disguise.

Mulder saw their eyes light up when he told them what had happened.

"I was in Franklin, Pennsylvania," Mulder said. "It was early morning. I was running. I needed the exercise and I needed to clear my mind. I'm on a case down there that—but I won't go into the details. Instead I'll get to the point of my visit."

"Do that," said Byers.

"Yes, do," agreed Langly.

"You know we're always eager to help," said Frohike. "Even though you work for the government."

"We know you won't be there forever," Byers declared. "You make too many waves. Someday they'll come to their senses and get rid of you. Or else you'll come to your senses and come work with us. There's always a place for you here, Fox, old boy."

"Not to mention your partner," said Frohike. "Where is Scully, anyway?"

"Training new recruits at the academy." Mulder said. "But I'm sure you don't want to talk about Scully when you could be talking about flies," he added with a smile.

"Hmmm," said Frohike. "Flies. What about them?"

"As I said, I was jogging along, one early morning, when a passenger truck with a camper shell in the back went by," Mulder said. "A hand reached out and let loose a bunch of small black specks. As the truck drove out of sight, I checked them out. They were flies, hundreds of them, crawling around the ground. Here's one I picked up."

Mulder reached into his pocket and produced

the specimen in a plastic bag. It hadn't survived the trip. He shook it out onto a tabletop.

"One more thing," he said. "The truck had an emblem on its side. It belonged to the city government."

That was all Byers, Langly, and Frohike needed to hear to cluster around the fly. Mulder could almost see their brains working.

Taking turns, they examined the fly through a high-powered magnifying glass.

"In the April issue of our newsletter," Byers told Mulder, "we ran an article on the CIA's latest miniature video camera. Model CCDTH7321, to be exact."

"It's small enough to put on the back of a fly," said Langly.

"Sounds intriguing. Imagine being one of those flies on the wall of the president's Oval Office," said Mulder.

"I don't have to imagine," Frohike said with a smirk. "I've done it."

"So is this fly equipped for surveillance?" asked Mulder.

"Unfortunately, no," said Frohike.

Byers thumbed through a reference book.

"This is a Eurasian cluster fly," he announced. "They infest vegetation, often fruit, like apples and cherries. They can cause a great deal of damage."

"You said you were in Franklin, Agent Mulder," said Langly. "They grow a lot of fruit around there. Maybe this fly was irradiated to control insects in the area. A safer method than pesticides. A dose of radiation makes the flies unable to reproduce. Then they're loose among the normal flies. In time they yank the fuse out of the fly population bomb."

"Hey, wait a minute," said Byers eagerly. "Here's another explanation. Maybe agents of competing South American agricultural countries, posing as Franklin city employees, are releasing fertile flies to destroy the crops."

"Sorry, Byers, but Langly is right," said Frohike, who had been examining the fly more closely. "Irradiation is the answer. This fly's been nuked."

Mulder patted Byers on the back. "Good try, though," he said.

"Any other little problems you want solved?" said Langly smugly.

"There is one more thing," Mulder said. He opened his briefcase and took out a paper.

"This is an FBI lab chemical analysis," he told them. "Know anything about this substance?"

Byers, Langly, and Frohike glanced at the report. They snickered.

"Obviously you did not read the August issue of our newsletter," said Byers.

"Sorry, boys," said Mulder. "It arrived on the same day as my copy of *Popular Science*."

"Come over here," said Byers.

Mulder followed Byers to a table cluttered with videos. His gazed flicked over the titles. *The J.F.K. Assassination. The Bobby Kennedy Assassination. The Martin Luther King, Jr., Assassination. Nixon, Volume I. Nixon, Volume II. Irangate. The October Surprise. The C.I.A. The F.B.I.*

Mulder picked up *The F.B.I.*

"Anything I should know?" he asked.

"Nothing you probably don't already suspect," said Byers, still hunting for the video he wanted. Then he said, "Here it is. *Toxic Pesticides*."

Byers put the video in a VCR.

Before he turned it on, he told Mulder, "The chemical in your report is lysergic dimethrin. It's an unreleased experimental insecticide designed to act as a pheromone."

"A pheromone?" Mulder queried. "That's a fear-inducing agent, right?"

"Right," Langly chimed in. "This LSDM is sprayed on a plant. It invokes a fear response in the pest. 'Get out of here. There's danger,' it says to the insect. The insect reacts and hightails out of there."

"Sounds good," said Mulder.

"Insecticides always sound good, if you listen to the folks who make them," said Langly.

"But you said they won't release it," said Mulder.

"They're not allowed to," said Langly. "Unless a government review lets them, which well may happen."

"Is it possible it may affect humans in a harmful manner?" asked Mulder.

"Possible? Take a look at this," said Byers. He turned on the video.

They saw a black-and-white newsreel of a truck cruising a suburban neighborhood. The truck was spraying thick clouds of chemical everywhere, over lawns, gardens, shrubs. A scene followed showing a worker spraying thick jets of chemical onto laughing, splashing children in a swimming pool. After that came a plane releasing vast quantities over farmlands and forests.

"This film is from the 1950s," said Langly. "The chemical being released is DDT. It was an insecticide that the government *did* decide was safe and let loose everywhere."

"Later they found out that people exposed to it had sharply higher rates of cancer," added Byers. "Not to mention whole species of wildlife that were nearly destroyed."

"The government later admitted a mistake had been made," Langly said.

"But by that time the chemical companies already had the profits in the bank—ready to be invested in the next generation of insecticides," said Byers, snapping off the video.

"Any more questions, Agent Mulder?" Langly said.

"Just for Frohike," said Mulder, who spotted Frohike tinkering with a pair of goggles. "Are those what I think they are?"

"Fresh out of the box—I'm just upgrading them," said Frohike.

He held up the box. A label read: LITTON M909 HIGH PERFORMANCE NIGHT GOGGLES.

"Can I borrow them?" Mulder asked.

"If you give me Scully's phone number," Frohike said.

Mulder looked at him indignantly.

"You really think I would compromise my partner's private life for a pair of goggles?"

Chapter ELEVEN

Mulder had to admit, the night goggles were good. They looked like simple binoculars. But even on a night with only a few twinkling stars, he could see orchards and farmhouses in the countryside around him. The world might look dark green and grainy, but objects in it were distinct.

Mulder was sitting on the hood of his rented car outside Franklin. He had been waiting there for two hours, by the side of a road cutting through the fruit orchards. So far he had seen nothing suspicious.

He still saw nothing. But he did hear something.

A faint rumbling in the distance.

When he had heard that rumbling nights ago in the sheriff's office, it had sounded like distant thunder.

Now it sounded like some kind of monstrous fly.

Or else a chopper with muffled engines.

His eyes pressed to the goggles, Mulder scanned the sky.

Above the treeline to the west, he saw it—the black shape of a helicopter moving fast. From it, like mist from a waterfall, came a cloud of spray.

Mulder dashed into his car. He laid the goggles beside him on the seat, next to his camera. He roared off toward where he had seen the spray descend.

When he got there, all was quiet. There was no sign that anything had happened.

Mulder snapped off his car lights. He got out of the car, night goggles in one hand, camera in the other.

He walked among the apple trees. Fruit hung heavy on the boughs, waiting to be harvested.

He reached up and pulled off an apple from a low bough. Eating it, though, was the last thing he wanted to do. Eve herself couldn't have tempted him to taste it. A lab analysis would tell what now was coating its skin, but he could make a good guess.

He wanted more evidence, though. In cases like this, you couldn't have too much proof. He wanted a shot of the chopper in the act.

Where had it gone? Was it finished for the night?

He strained his ears. He heard nothing.

He peered into the black sky through the goggles. Still nothing.

Shoulders slumped, Mulder started walking back to his car. Another night, maybe. There would surely be one.

Then, from behind him, a rumbling swept the night.

Above his head, branches, leaves and apples trembled.

Mulder dropped to the ground, making himself into a human ball.

But there was no hiding from the dark mist that rained down, covering him.

Mulder choked, gasping for air.

His last thought before he blacked out was that he didn't have to collect evidence anymore.

He *was* evidence.

County Supervisor Larry Winter tried to deny everything.

"Stealth helicopters?" he said. "Experimental pesticides? And all this the cause of violent behavior? Look, Agent Mulder, I'm sorry you had some kind of little accident. But it seems to have affected your mind. You are fantasizing."

"I tell you, I saw the helicopter with my own eyes—from two different locations," said Mulder angrily, trying to sit up in his hospital bed.

Sheriff Spencer stepped to Winter's side, in case Mulder tried something violent. The G-man looked a bit unstable.

But Spencer did not have to worry. A hand gently but firmly pushed Mulder down.

"Cool it, partner," Scully told him. "I'm set to take another blood sample."

Mulder grunted as she stuck another needle in his arm.

"You've already taken enough blood to float a blood bank," he complained.

"Sorry, Mulder, but I want to run some backup tests."

Scully capped the vial of blood and put it on a table. In science you could never be too sure of anything. Besides, in this case, the more tests she ran, the more proof she had that she was needed here. Even when the news that Mulder was in the hospital hit FBI headquarters, it hadn't been easy to get approval to join him in Franklin. Scully had had to warn the brass what might happen if the accident made Mulder lose control. They had no problem believing that he might go over the edge. In fact, it was one of their nightmares.

Actually, Scully hadn't been far off the mark. Right now Mulder was . . . agitated.

"Look at my hair!" he told Winter. "Feel my skin! The insecticide is still on me."

Winter responded with cool contempt. "I've checked up on you, Agent Mulder. I've heard about you and your spooky ideas. You're in Franklin, Pennsylvania. Not Mars."

"Don't try to shift blame," said Mulder. "Don't

act like a victim of unjust suspicion when others are dead."

Winter glared at Mulder. "Hold it just a second. Remember who you're talking to."

"I know whom I'm talking to," Mulder said. "I'm talking to a man responsible for illegal spraying. The sooner you admit it, the sooner people will stop dying. The killers all lived near heavily sprayed areas."

Mulder and Winter locked gazes. Scully could almost see sparks fly.

"You don't live here, Mulder," Winter said. "I live here. I have my heart in this town. I have three children here. I'm not going to dump poison on them."

"If the spraying is so safe, why was it done in secret?" Mulder demanded.

"I don't know what kind of crusade you're on," said Winter. "Do you work for the FBI or some save-the-whales-and-spotted-owls environmental group?"

Suddenly Spencer spoke. He had been standing silent, listening. Now his voice was harsh.

"Answer the question, Larry," he said. "Are we spraying?"

There was a loud silence. Then Winter cleared his throat and said defiantly, "This county lives on money from its fruit harvest. If the crops fail, so do the farms around here, the stores, the banks, everything. Where will people find work? How do they house, clothe, feed themselves and their kids?"

He was met by stony silence.

"Insects threatened every tree in the area," he argued. "The irradiated flies we tried weren't working fast enough. And the delays to get government approval of the spray would have caused total crop damage. People's lives would have been ruined by those lousy bugs."

"Ruined?" said Spencer, shaking his head. "Twenty-three people are dead."

"There is no proof whatsoever that the spray is causing violent behavior," Winter said. "It was proven to be safe."

"By whom?" Mulder said, sitting up in the bed. "Who proved it to you and how?"

"The manufacturer gave me the results of a three-year study," Winter said.

"What kind of study?" asked Mulder.

"On laboratory rats," Winter said. "A common procedure."

"Except that humans are often a bit different than rats—in some ways at least," Mulder said, staring hard at Winter.

"Studies on humans are being planned—thanks to environmentalists and other cranks like you,"

Winter said. "There is no reason, though, to suspect the results will be any different. And as I said, it will delay the use of this valuable tool for years."

"Instead you've turned the people around here into human guinea pigs," said Mulder. "More than that, you've turned them into victims."

"I will not accept responsibility for anything that is not demonstrated to be doing harm," said Winter. "And I defy you to prove that LSDM does any of the things you claim."

Mulder turned to Scully.

Before he could ask her to back him up, she said, "He's right, Mulder."

Mulder's mouth fell open.

"Sorry, Mulder," Scully went on. "I wish I could say I flew three hundred miles in the middle of the night to perform tests that proved you are about to become the next mass murderer. But I find no evidence that LSDM has seriously affected you. Even after you had a massive dose of it."

"But, Scully, your own autopsy reported that the last killer had chemical abnormalities," Mulder protested.

"Yes—and you do not," Scully said. "You are living proof they were not from exposure to LSDM."

Mulder slumped back in the bed. Stunned, he stared at the ceiling, trying to think.

But all he could think of was the television set that hung from the ceiling.

Mulder had snapped off the sound when his visitors arrived, but the set was still on.

Now his gaze was drawn as if by a magnet to the screen.

He could not turn his eyes away from the message that shone there in burning red:

DO IT!

His eyes widened as the print got larger and the message grew stronger.

DO IT NOW!

Chapter TWELVE

Mulder stared at the message on the TV screen. His teeth clenched. His hands tightened into fists. Then he went limp, though his face was still beaded with sweat.

The message had vanished. In its place a young woman in spandex workout gear was doing aerobics with a dazzling smile on her face.

Still staring at the screen, Mulder groped for the TV remote on his bedside table. He turned on the sound.

"Yes, do it," an announcer's voice boomed out. "Do it now—before our special offer of half-price membership in Franklin's newest and most up-to-date health club runs out."

Mulder turned off the set. But he continued to stare at the screen.

Mulder knew that you never could predict when or where a solution to a case would appear. He only knew that in the depths of your mind, everything you saw and heard in an investigation was processed like data in a computer. Then something pressed the right key and you saw it all clearly.

"Scully, are you familiar with subliminal messages?" asked Mulder.

"Huh?" said Larry Winter.

Scully, though, took Mulder's remark in stride. She was used to his pitches coming in from left field.

"Subliminal messages?" she said. "Sure. Some people claim that advertisers deliver messages hidden in their regular ads. Messages that you don't realize you're seeing or hearing. Messages that slip through your defenses to punch the buttons in your brain. They can be words spelled out in ice cubes. Or voices masked by ear-splitting music. Or other deceitful devices."

"Right," said Mulder.

"Mulder, the people who think they are being bombarded by subliminal messages are the same people who think that everything is part of a gigantic conspiracy against them," said Scully. "Like your pals the Lone Gunmen."

"Scully," Mulder said. "Some department stores insert subliminal messages in their wall-to-wall music to discourage shoplifting. And they are not the only ones. The technique is widely used and it is effective."

Scully sighed. "Okay. The technique is used. But what does it have to do with the LSDM spraying?"

"Electronic devices were destroyed by every killer," Mulder said.

"Still waiting for an explanation," said Scully.

"The insecticide, LSDM, is known to produce a fear response in cluster flies," Mulder went on. "What if the chemical creates the same reaction in humans?"

"That's open to doubt," Scully said. "A great many people doubtless received heavy doses of the spray. Only a handful became killers."

"Perhaps only those under severe stress are adversely affected by the chemical," said Mulder. "We know that stress weakens the body's defenses against disease. It may weaken defenses against LSDM. Certainly we know that the last two killers had pressing job and money problems."

"Shoot," said Sheriff Spencer. "Most everyone in town is stressed out that way—what with the crops in danger, plus companies downsizing."

"Right," said Supervisor Winter. "Franklin is turning into Stress City."

Mulder was not to be stopped or even slowed down. "Let us say that the chemical can tip the balance only when a person harbors a strong fear above and beyond common stress," he said. "We know from friends and family as well as the elevator massacre survivors that closed spaces made

Gary Taber extremely uncomfortable. A therapist he once saw terms him a borderline claustrophobic. We also know from Bonnie McRoberts's husband and coworkers that she harbored a fear of male dominance and antifemale discrimination that amounted to an obsession. Do you agree?"

"I agree," Spencer said. Scorn had faded from the sheriff's face as he listened to Mulder.

"I am not listening to any more of this," said Winter. "You don't belong in a hospital room, Mulder. You belong in a padded cell. Believe me, I'm going to let your superiors know what kind of loose cannon they have careening around the country."

With that he strode out of the room, slamming the door behind him.

Meanwhile, Spencer kept his eyes on Mulder. "So where is all this leading?" the sheriff demanded.

"The insecticide heightened their fear to a point where it overrode everything else," said Mulder. "With that fear in control, they became responsive to messages that told them what to do with their fear."

"A pretty far-out theory," said Spencer. "It leaves a lot of blank spots. Like exactly how fear turns into murder."

"That can be chemically explained," Mulder said. He turned to his partner.

"Am I right to say that adrenaline is called the 'fight or flight' hormone, Agent Scully?" he inquired. "That is, it is produced by either fear or anger. In turn, it fuels either fear or anger."

Scully nodded. "That's right," she said. "A good example is a cornered rat. It will either desperately try to climb the wall to escape, or it will viciously attack."

Mulder turned back to Spencer. "Fear floods the body with adrenaline. To use that adrenaline to inflame rage is a matter of throwing a switch. I believe that someone wanted to see if a combination of LSDM and subliminal messaging could throw that switch—and on whom it would work. I believe those messages were deliberately sent after this area was sprayed."

"But, Mulder," said Scully softly. "Who did it?"

Mulder hesitated. He began to open his mouth to answer.

Before he could, Sheriff Spencer's mouth tightened. Without a word, the tall man turned and left the room.

"You've lost another one," Scully commented.

"Ahh," said Mulder. "He's probably one of those people who thinks Elvis is really dead."

Scully cleared her throat.

"Mulder," she said hesitantly. "I have a confession."

"Confess by all means."

"I was wrong," Scully said.

"Oh?" said Mulder.

"You've convinced me," Scully said. "You, and evidence I cannot dismiss. Exposure to the insecticide can and probably does cause insane fear. Paranoia."

"Perhaps then you can share my belief as well that this area is being subjected to a controlled experiment," Mulder said.

"Controlled by whom?" Scully said. "The government? A corporation? Aliens?"

"Hard to say—but it's been done before," said Mulder. "Agent Orange in Vietnam. DDT in the United States. Germ warfare experiments on unsuspecting neighborhoods and even in the New York City subways. Radiation experiments in vast stretches of the West."

"But in this case, why?" asked Scully. "Why would anyone intentionally create a breed of killers in the general population."

"Fear," said Mulder. "It's the oldest tool of power. If you are distracted by the fear of the people around you, you stop paying attention to the actions of those above you. In times of hardship, with more and more people getting mad at politicians and corporations, this kind of distraction is useful for those running the show. By changing fear to anger in a few, they can change anger to fear in all the rest."

Scully's brow furrowed as she followed Mulder's reasoning.

"So what do you say, Scully?" he asked her.

At that moment the door of the hospital room opened.

Sheriff Spencer walked in. His face was grim.

"I've had a talk with Mr. Winter," he said. "I've persuaded him to a compromise—after I suggested his upcoming election campaign would not be helped if I made certain disclosures to the news media."

"My compliments," said Mulder. "You're the professional investigator I hoped you might be." Mulder paused and braced himself before asking, "Tell me, what is the compromise?"

"He has agreed to stop the spraying immediately," Spencer said. "He has also agreed to blood testing of people exposed in the sprayed areas. But . . ." He paused.

"But . . . ?" Mulder asked.

"But—the official explanation for the blood testing cannot mention any link to the possible side effects of LSDM," said Spencer. His face had the expression of someone swallowing a bitter pill.

Mulder and Scully looked at each other.

It was business as usual.

Chapter THIRTEEN

Larry Winter had struck a hard bargain.

But at least he kept his part of it. And he did so with an efficiency that Mulder and Scully had to acknowledge.

"Maybe the guy doesn't always do the right thing," Scully said to Mulder. "But at least he knows how to get things done."

Two days later the citywide blood testing program began. A center was set up at the local community college. Citizens could come there to have their blood analyzed. For those who did not want to make the trip, blood testing teams spread over the city. And to make sure the news went out, the campaign was announced in the morning and afternoon papers and around the clock on local TV.

"Believe me, nobody in town will escape our media blitz," Winter told Mulder and Scully.

He was right.

No one could escape. Not even a man who had locked his doors and drawn his curtains and cowered inside his house for days.

Ed Funsch's eyes were glazed with exhaustion

as he sat in the shabby living room of his run-down house and watched cartoons on a TV he hadn't finished paying for. He needed a good night's sleep. But he couldn't get one. He tossed and turned in bed, plagued by visions of violence. If only they were nightmares. But they came to him while he was still awake. At least when he saw Daffy Duck and Road Runner bash and trash each other, he knew it was all a joke.

Suddenly Daffy vanished from the screen, just as he ran smack into a brick wall.

An announcer's voice said, "We interrupt this program to bring you a special message from your local government."

A printed announcement appeared: FREE CHOLESTEROL TESTING. At your own home, or at a special bloodmobile on Franklin Community College campus, 1505 North Franklin Avenue."

Ed squinted at the screen. Where had Daffy and Road Runner gone? Why was Ed being yanked back into the real world when it was the last place he wanted to be?

The TV voice explained: "Franklin and Venango counties are participating in an important nationwide study of cholesterol. It is essential that every citizen join in the fight against this cause of deadly disease. When one of our trained volunteers comes to your door, please cooperate fully. The procedure is simple and painless. And the life you help save may be your own."

A picture appeared on the screen, and suddenly Ed was wide awake.

He saw a fingertip appear. Then a needle went into it. It drew a tiny bit of blood.

"Just a little needle prick on your fingertip—that's all there is to it," the TV voice said soothingly. "Your help will be appreciated by your government, family, friends, and neighbors."

Ed didn't hear a word.

All he could see was the blood.

All he could see was red.

His hand fell to the coffee table in front of him. He felt something cold. He looked down. His palm was on the barrel of a hunting rifle in an open carrying case.

Where had the weapon come from? And the boxes of cartridges next to it?

Then he remembered what he wanted to forget. The Superstore. The barrage of TV messages hitting him. The shopping spree in the gun department.

Beside the gun and cartridges lay the sales receipt. With it were his checkbook and a pocket calculator. He double-checked the numbers. They came out the way he was afraid they would. Buying the gun had cleaned out his bank account.

"And I hate guns, too," he muttered to himself. "I must have been out of my skull. Too much strain lately. Maybe I can return the stuff and get my dough back. I'll do that, when I start feeling better."

He looked back at the TV and grumbled, "Why don't they end that fool announcement? Who cares about that cholesterol stuff, whatever it is? They should put Daffy back on."

The doorbell rang.

Ed grimaced. "Who's that? Why won't they let me alone? Give me some peace and quiet? That's all I want."

He went to the window and peeked out between the curtains.

A young woman in a white lab coat stood at his front door. She wore a cheerful smile and latex medical gloves. She carried a small leather kit.

Ed knew what was in that kit.

A needle. A needle that drew blood.

He closed the curtain tight. She mustn't know anyone was home. He heard the TV behind him, the announcer droning on and on.

"So once again, when you hear your doorbell ring, we urge you to—"

Ed turned and raced for the TV, his hand poised to turn it off.

He froze.

A single word covered the screen.

BLOOD

His hand swept down and knocked the TV off its stand. It hit the floor with a crash, the screen going dark.

The woman outside must have heard the noise. The doorbell rang again.

Ed shut his eyes and put his hands over his ears. Why didn't that young woman go away? Why didn't everything just go away? Why didn't the world stop closing in, driving him into a corner?

But the ringing still filtered through, distant and broken up. It came to him like some kind of Morse code, spelling out a message he couldn't decipher yet somehow had to obey.

He saw his hands reaching for the hunting rifle.

"No!" he cried, slamming the case shut.

The impact knocked the pocket calculator off the coffee table.

Automatically he stooped to pick it up.

As he lifted it, he read its display.

TAKE THEIRS

Ed smashed the calculator on the tabletop. Again and again and again. Its parts spilled out from its shattered plastic casing.

The doorbell rang again.

It set off another sound—a sharp, irritating beeping.

Where was it coming from?

In a moment Ed found it.

It came from the cheap digital watch on his wrist.

The beeping watch was flashing on and off like a neon sign.

Blinking, Ed read it through tears of torment and rage.

KILL. KILL. KILL.

Chapter FOURTEEN

Mulder and Scully turned Sheriff Spencer's office into their headquarters. From it they followed the progress of the blood testing campaign.

On the bulletin board was a large map of Franklin and the area around it. Next to it was a list of areas that had been sprayed. Beside that was a list of the names and addresses of the people who lived in those areas.

Sheriff Spencer stood by the phone, taking calls from the blood testing teams. All day they had been phoning in reports of their progress. As the names of people tested came in, Spencer scribbled them down, then passed the information to Scully. Scully then crossed off those names from the list on the bulletin board. When everyone in a neighborhood was accounted for, that neighborhood was crossed off the other list.

Mulder quietly stood by and watched Scully enjoying herself. She was never happier than when things went according to plan.

Sheriff Spencer hung up the phone, handed Scully the latest batch of names, and said, "That's it. The last area just reported in."

Scully crossed the names off the list. Mulder and Spencer joined her in looking over the results.

"A pretty good job, if I do say so myself," Spencer said. "Everyone except a handful of people has been tested."

"Twenty-five people untested, to be exact," said Scully.

"Well, there's always a few kooks and cranks who won't go along with the crowd," said Spencer.

"Right, kooks and cranks," said Mulder, looking closely at the remaining names.

Scully smiled. The sheriff had said the magic words. Anything and anyone that departed from the norm was right up Mulder's alley.

"We've finished the easy part of the job—now things may start getting interesting," Mulder said. He checked the automatic in his shoulder holster. "They also may get a little messy." He put on his jacket. "Let's go. We have twenty-five visits to make."

Scully checked her gun, then picked up a blood testing kit.

Spencer merely patted the gun in the holster on his belt.

Their first stop was at the home of Mrs. Henrietta Smith.

She screamed that she wasn't buying anything. It

took twenty minutes to convince her that this wasn't going to cost her a penny. And the only reason she believed that was that Mulder seemed such a nice young man. He reminded her of her favorite nephew.

The next stop was Robert Jones's house. He had a steel front door. He shouted through a mail slot that he wasn't letting any commie fascist government officials intrude in his life, not after the Waco massacre.

Scully was able to talk him into opening his door. A good citizen like Mr. Jones wanted to serve the cause of medical science, didn't he? And a big strong man like him wasn't scared of a little old needle, was he? Her smile, along with her words, finally did the trick.

Next was Mr. Hiram Phelps. He kept insisting he had given at the office. It took a flash of Spencer's badge to make him see reason.

By the time they reached the fourteenth name on the list, it seemed they had hit every possible kind of roadblock.

They were wrong.

"Who's this guy?" asked Spencer as they approached the front door of a beat-up little house on the seedy edge of town. Mulder took note of its location—it was across from a garbage dump and next to a cherry orchard.

Scully consulted her list.

"A Mr. Edward Funsch," she said.

Scully reached out to press the doorbell.

At her touch the metal plate around the buzzer fell onto the doormat.

Mulder came forward to take a look at the exposed buzzer.

"Somebody yanked away the plate and pulled the buzzer out by the wires," he said. "Then the person stuffed it all back so it couldn't be easily spotted."

"Maybe an angry Girl Scout who couldn't unload her cookies," said Scully.

"Or else a man who has a serious problem with visitors," said Mulder.

"One way to find out," said Spencer, and he knocked on the door.

No answer.

After a minute Scully said, "I believe we are legally justified to attempt entrance on probable suspicion of foul play."

"Sam Jenkins, the local judge, will buy that," said Spencer.

Scully turned the front doorknob.

"It's unlocked," she said. "I see people really trust their neighbors here in Franklin."

"That's the way it used to be," Spencer said. "But right now, I don't figure anyone in town is leaving front doors unlocked. Anyone in his right mind, anyway."

Spencer's hand hovered over his pistol butt as Mulder swung the door open.

With Mulder leading the way, the three of them entered the house as if walking into a minefield.

But the explosion already seemed to have happened.

"What hit this dump?" Spencer wondered aloud as they inspected the damage.

A television set lay smashed on the living room floor. Beside it were the remains of a digital watch. In the kitchen was the wreckage of a microwave oven and a radio, as well as another smashed mini-TV.

"Look at this," said Scully from a hallway, where a vacuum cleaner lay, destroyed.

"Some maniac must have gotten loose," said Spencer.

"If so, there was a method to the madness," said Mulder. "Do you notice that every single smashed object has something in common?"

"What's that?" asked Spencer.

"Every one of them has an electronic digital display," said Mulder.

"Let's go over the house again to make sure," Scully said.

But when they returned to the living room, Mulder noticed something else in the room's debris: a carrying case. For a hunting rifle.

He opened it. It was empty.

Chapter FIFTEEN

"We have to find out all we can about this Edward Funsch," Mulder said, staring at the empty rifle case. "And we have to do it fast."

"I'll see what I can dig up on the Internet—and the bureau data bank," said Scully. "He must be in the files of someone somewhere. Everyone is."

"I'll ask around town about him," Spencer offered.

"I'll keep on searching the house," Mulder said. "Come back with whatever you can find."

Forty minutes later Scully and Spencer arrived back at the house at the same time.

Mulder read aloud the printout that Scully handed him. "Edward Funsch. Fifty-two years old. Born and raised in Pittsburgh, Pennsylvania. Graduated high school but no college degree. Served in the navy as a radioman. His wife died ten years ago. No children. No car or driver's license. No medical history. No record of a doctor or dentist visit for decades. Worked in an airplane factory for twelve years but was laid off after a corporate merger and personnel downsizing. Worked for the Postal Service for several months, but very recently was laid off from that job. Almost nothing in the bank. Rent and credit card payments overdue."

Mulder turned to Spencer. "Did you learn anything about him?"

"Not much to learn," said Spencer. "He had no police record. He belonged to no local organizations. He had no close friends and little to do with neighbors. He was a good but not an exceptional worker at the Postal Service, and was fired for reasons that had nothing to do with job performance."

"How did he react to his firing?" asked Mulder. "Did he show any strong signs of anger?"

"Hard to say," said Spencer. "I talked to his job supervisor on the phone. He said that Ed seemed to take the bad news okay, though naturally he wasn't too happy. But he acted more bothered by a paper cut he had on his finger than by being cut from the payroll. It was just a little nick, but apparently the sight of blood really shook him up. His boss found that pretty strange."

Mulder stiffened. "Scully," he said, "do we know when the blood tester rang Ed Funsch's doorbell?"

Scully consulted her list. "About ten-thirty this morning," she said.

Mulder picked up the wristwatch he had found smashed on the living room floor.

It was stopped at 10:25 A.M.

"I know what he's afraid of," said Mulder. "And I have a good idea where he's going."

Ed Funsch knew where he had to go and was in a desperate hurry to get there.

The bus was just pulling away when he arrived at the stop.

An electronic display flashed its destination: FRANKLIN COMMUNITY MEDICAL CENTER.

It flashed a different message to Ed:

GET ABOARD.

He dashed after it, moving like a sprinter. A big gym carryall swung from his shoulder and bounced against his side as he tore down the sidewalk, one fist banging against the side of the bus.

The bus driver knew he shouldn't stop. He was behind schedule already. With recent cutbacks in bus service, he had to drive his route faster than ever before. His job performance rating was tied to his on-time record—and the drivers who rated worst were laid off first.

But the driver was only human. He had to take pity on the poor clown running beside the bus. He put on the brakes and opened the door. He wished he hadn't when Ed clambered aboard.

"Fare, mister," the driver said as Ed headed past him toward the rear.

Ed gave him a blank look. Then he blinked dully and fumbled for the right change. He dropped it into the fare box and went on his way.

By that time the driver had gotten a good look at Ed's face. It was pale, almost green. Sweat beaded the skin. And mingling with the sweat were streaks of tears.

The driver sighed. He'd better keep an eye on this guy in his rearview mirror. The last thing the driver needed was trouble. Too many delays, and a pink slip would be waiting at the end of the line.

But Ed sat quietly in the middle of the bus, not bothering any of the other passengers. He didn't even look at them. All he was looking at was the STOP REQUESTED electronic display in the front of the bus.

Suddenly the display told Ed: GET OFF HERE!

Ed jumped to his feet as if hit by a cattle prod. In three giant steps he was at the side exit door.

He pressed the Stop Request button.

The bus kept moving.

"Hey, driver, I want to get off," Ed shouted.

The driver didn't bother turning his head.

"You have to wait for the next bus stop," he said, his voice barely reaching Ed.

"Where's that?" shouted Ed.

"Fifteen blocks," the driver said. "This bus makes express stops only."

"Please, I'm on the wrong bus," Ed pleaded.

"Sorry, mister, I don't make the rules," the driver replied.

"But I tell you, I have to get off," Ed said, his voice rising to a scream.

"And I tell you, tough luck," the driver replied, an angry edge to his voice.

Ed half ran, half stumbled to the front of the swaying bus as it sped down the road.

"Driver, *please*, *please*," he said, leaning forward so that the driver had to see his face.

The driver got an eyeful. This guy was practically frothing at the mouth.

"Open the door!" Ed's voice blasted into the driver's ear. "Open the dag-blamed door!"

"Hey, mister, relax, okay?" the driver said with a touch of panic.

He slammed on the brakes. The bus came to a screeching halt. The door opened. And Ed was out in a flash.

The driver closed the door almost as fast and started off again.

He wiped the sweat from his forehead, focused on the road ahead, and tried to relax.

Let somebody else worry about that nut, he thought.

Chapter SIXTEEN

"This is where the blood winds up," Mulder told Scully and Spencer. "If blood is what he fears, blood is what he wants to destroy."

Mulder was explaining why they were waiting at the bus stop at the Franklin Community Medical Center.

"Since Funsch doesn't have a driver's license or a car, a bus is the natural way for him to go," he added.

Scully turned to a man standing at the bus stop with them. He wore a city transportation department uniform and carried a clipboard.

"Do you happen to know when the next bus is due?" she asked.

"I sure do, ma'am. Three minutes ago," the man growled, checking his watch. "That driver is going to have some explaining to do."

"Here it comes," said Spencer as the bus turned a corner and headed for the stop.

"The guy is driving too fast, too," the bus inspector muttered, making a notation on his clipboard.

The bus arrived and the doors opened. Mulder

watched the passengers as they stepped off the bus, comparing them to the photo of Ed Funsch he'd found at Ed's house.

None of them looked like Ed.

"We'll quiz the driver," he told Scully.

Before they could enter the bus, though, the driver came out.

"Do you recognize this man?" Mulder asked him, showing the man Ed Funsch's photo.

"Sure do," said the driver. He turned to the inspector. "I had a real problem with this guy," he said. "He acted totally crazy. Demanded to be let off before the proper stop. I had to do it, or he might have hurt somebody. That's why I'm late."

"Sure," said the inspector. "There's always some excuse."

"But I tell you—" the driver started to say.

"Where did this man want to be let off?" Scully cut in.

"Right near the college," said the driver, resuming his explanation to the inspector.

Mulder and Scully didn't bother listening to the rising voices of the two men. They started walking toward Spencer's squad car with him.

"I was wrong," Mulder said with a grimace. "It wasn't the hospital Ed Funsch wanted to get to. It was the bloodmobile at the college."

"It sounds like a likely target," Scully agreed.

Sheriff Spencer's face was grim as he thought of the testing center he had helped set up on the campus.

"Yeah, a likely target," he said. "Complete with sitting ducks."

Ed Funsch took in the entire scene at a glance.

The bloodmobile was parked in the center of a large open courtyard on the campus. Outside the van, attendants sat behind a large folding table, where forms were filled out. A long line of men, women, and children waited their turn to be tested. Franklin had more than its share of good citizens, wanting to do their duty in the war against disease. Brightly colored balloons were strung on light poles.

Ed admired all these people for their bravery in actually giving their blood for the good of others.

At the same time, he pitied them for the pain they would have to endure.

The publicity talked about a little pinprick. Ed knew better. He shuddered, drenched in cold sweat.

Through a mist of revulsion, he saw an electronic sign set up for students, listing the day's events.

CAMPUS EVENTS TODAY . . . LECTURE ON MEDIEVAL HISTORY, SAMUELSON HALL 4 P.M. . . . CHEERLEADING TRYOUTS, KELLY FIELD, 5 P.M. . . . BASKETBALL . . .

College must be nice, Ed thought. He would have liked to go to college. Maybe if he had gone to college, things would be different. Maybe—

Then he saw the words for his eyes only:

UP . . . LOOK UP

Ed looked up.

He saw the bell tower that loomed over the courtyard.

GO FOR IT said the sign.

Like a sleepwalker, Ed approached the door of the tower and opened it. Before him winding stairs led upward. One by one he climbed them, moving slowly, heavily, as if the gym bag he carried weighed a hundred pounds.

At the top of the tower was a circular room. Tall, slotlike windows ran around it.

Panting, Ed laid down his bag, then looked out a window. He saw the ivy-covered buildings of the college, ablaze with sunlight. He saw the long line of people waiting snakelike in front of the bloodmobile. The sight made him want to weep even more. But instead he read the words moving by on the electronic sign.

GET READY . . . GET READY . . . GET READY they told him again and again until finally he obeyed and unzipped the gym bag.

He pulled out the hunting rifle. Then he turned

the bag over and emptied out the rest of the contents. Hundreds of full metal cartridges clattered onto the cold stone floor.

Ed stuffed handfuls of cartridges into his pockets, then he carried the rifle to the window overlooking the courtyard. The sign there flashed at him like a beacon.

GET SET.

He knelt by the window. Propping his elbow on the ledge, he pointed the rifle downward. He snapped off the safety catch. He inserted a round into the firing chamber. He cocked the bolt. His finger rested on the icy trigger as he squinted through the rifle sights.

Suddenly he froze. He heard a loud wailing coming closer and closer.

He recognized the sound. A police siren.

Terror filled him.

They were coming for him!

What should he do?

He looked at the sign. The answer to his question flashed at him:

DO IT!

Chapter SEVENTEEN

Spencer's squad car skidded to a stop in the campus courtyard.

Mulder flung open the door and was out instantly, running toward the bloodmobile. Scully and Spencer were right behind.

He heard Scully gasp, "If only we can get there in time."

He heard a sharp crack in the air.

He saw a window on the bloodmobile shatter.

The people waiting in line looked around, puzzled.

There was another shot.

Spinters flew from the table in front of the bloodmobile. A volunteer sitting at it put her hand to her face. It came away covered with blood from a splinter cut. Her mouth opened silently; she was too shocked to make a sound.

Another shot rang out—followed by a cry of pain from a man who clutched his arm.

Screams came from every side. The crowd milled around in the courtyard like a herd of sheep, not knowing what the danger was, where it came from, and where safety lay.

Mulder, Scully, and Spencer dashed for cover behind the bloodmobile.

"We're too late," Mulder said.

"Where is he?" asked Scully.

"From the shot that hit the bloodmobile, he has to be somewhere on the other side from where we are," said Mulder.

Another shot—and another cry of pain, this one from a woman.

"Maybe he'll run out of ammo," said Spencer.

"Not much chance," said Mulder. "There were two empty cartridge boxes at his place. He must have hundreds of rounds."

Another rifle shot.

Mulder's eyes swept the courtyard, hunting for the glint of a rifle in the bright afternoon sun.

He saw people hugging the ground, others standing frozen in panic. Some were praying; others wept. He saw two bodies lying motionless on the grass.

There was another shot, and a man on the ground twitched and then stopped moving altogether.

Still Mulder could see no sign of the weapon—until he looked skyward when the rifle fired again.

A light puff of smoke drifted from a slotlike window high in a bell tower.

Mulder ducked back behind the bloodmobile.

"Funsch is up in the bell tower," he told the others.

"I'll get to the squad car," said Spencer. "And I'll call for a backup."

"No time for that," Mulder said. "Just call for medical help."

Without waiting for a reply, he was off and running.

As he dashed across the courtyard, he heard the rifle again. But the bullet didn't come near him. A man cried out in pain ten feet away.

Mulder had a strong hunch that Funsch wasn't picking targets. He was firing in a blind rage.

Mulder reached the door of the bell tower and stood there for a moment, catching his breath. Then he opened the door, pulled out his gun, and headed up the stairs two at a time.

His breath was burning in his lungs and his calf muscles were two balls of pain when he reached the top.

He stared across the room at Ed Funsch's back. The floor where he stood was littered with ejected shells. His body gave a jerk as he fired once more. As the blast died, it was replaced by the sound of Ed's weeping.

Sobbing loudly, he reached into his pocket and pulled out another cartridge.

Mulder leveled his pistol. "Put the gun down, Ed! " he shouted. "Put it down!"

Ed turned slowly, his rifle pointed at the ceiling. He stared at Mulder with tear-reddened eyes.

"Don't kill me," he said softly, like a child without hope.

"Then put it down, Ed."

Ed started to cry again. "I can't," he choked. "They won't let me."

"I know they won't, Ed," Mulder said gently. "I know they won't let you."

"Then . . . you . . . you make me put it down," Ed said, and stared straight at Mulder's gun with a weary look on his face. It was the look of a man so tired that he would do anything to find rest.

Mulder met Ed's gaze and saw the pleading there. He felt the trigger underneath his finger. His mind searched desperately for another way out.

"If you don't put it down, Ed," Mulder said, "and if I have to shoot you, or if you shoot me, there's going to be blood everywhere. You don't want that, do you? Blood all over? Blood you can't get away from? Think about it. You don't want that, do you, Ed?"

As Ed got the picture his face relaxed, as if a huge weight had been removed from him. Smiling, he held the rifle out to Mulder.

Mulder felt a wave of relief go through him.

Smiling also, he lowered his pistol.

Then he reached out with his other hand to take the rifle.

As Mulder extended his hand, his jacket sleeve rode up, exposing his forearm. It was the forearm that Bonnie McRoberts had slashed. Mulder's wound must have opened again, for the gauze bandage that bound it was soaked with blood.

"Agghhh!" Ed screamed, made frantic by the sight of blood. Using his rifle as a club, he swung at Mulder's gun hand.

The pistol fell from Mulder's stunned fingers to the floor.

Mulder could do just one thing, and he did it.

He charged Ed Funsch, trying to wrestle the rifle from him.

Knowing adrenaline could give a man superhuman strength was one thing. Actually battling a man who was overdosing on adrenaline truly drove the lesson home.

Ed's vicious kick caught Mulder in the kneecap. As searing pain shot through his leg, Mulder struggled to keep his feet. Ed's savage shove threw Mulder off balance and smashed him against the wall. The back of Mulder's head crashed against concrete and stars danced in his eyes.

But Ed wasn't the only one flooded with adrenaline now.

A man fighting for his life had his own supply to tap.

Mulder felt it flowing through him as he gave Ed a hard push and at the same time gave the rifle a powerful twist.

Ed twisted it the other way and as they lurched across the floor like a pair of grunting bears locked in a clumsy dance.

Finally they stood struggling in the open doorway. At their feet the stairway fell away into darkness.

Mulder felt himself going over the edge of the top step.

With one last burst of strength, he pushed back.

With that same surge of power, he tore the rifle from Ed's hands.

In the same motion, he tossed it behind him to free his hands.

He heard the weapon clattering down the stairs as he forced Ed to his knees. He yanked Ed's arms behind his back and clicked handcuffs around Ed's wrists as Ed went limp with defeat or relief or both.

Chapter EIGHTEEN

"I want to give him a full examination," Scully said after the police took Ed Funsch away, strapped into a stretcher. "I don't expect to learn much more from him, though, than I did from the autopsies of the other killers. There's only so much that chemical analysis can tell you."

"We'll hold him in the hospital for as long as you want," Spencer said. "We'll keep him under armed guard."

"I don't think you'll have to watch him too closely," Mulder said. "All the fight seems to have gone out of him. Of course, you'll have to make sure there are no digital displays in the room. And Scully, when you take blood from him, make sure he doesn't see it."

The three of them were standing in front of the bell tower. The courtyard was empty, ringed by deputy sheriffs keeping out the curious. The TV camera crews had come and gone. All that remained was the bloodmobile with its shattered window, the table with its bullet marks, bright balloons bobbing on the evening breeze, and the banner reading

BLOOD. Only a very close look would have revealed brown spots of dried blood on the concrete walkway and the grass.

The peaceful scene was lit by a flaming sunset. As he had many times before, Mulder thought how much more there was in the world than the eye could see.

It was like watching a puppet show, he thought—a puppet show that people called reality. How he longed to shine the spotlight on the people pulling the strings.

He turned to Spencer. "I'll want unrestricted access to Ed Funsch for questioning."

"Sure, if you think that will get you anywhere," Spencer said. "But to tell the truth, Mulder, you already know more about what happened to him than he does."

"And I want to see Larry Winter, too," Mulder said. "I want to find out about the company that did the spraying."

"I already asked him about that," Spencer said. "Seems the company no longer exists. It was eliminated as of yesterday by the multinational that owns it. Some kind of corporate restructuring."

"I think I know where I can find out about that multinational," said Mulder. "I'll give them a call."

Scully smiled.

"Look, I have to get to the hospital now," she told Mulder. "But if you make that call to your informed source, give your friend Frohike a message from me."

"What's that?" asked Mulder.

"Tell him I've changed my telephone number."

Mulder watched Scully go off with Spencer, who had offered to drive her to the hospital.

Then Mulder walked to the bloodmobile and sat down in a folding chair. The wound in his arm ached, and every bruise on his body was throbbing. The sun had set now, and he shivered in the first chill of darkness. He took a tiny cellular phone from his pocket and punched out a number. He put the phone to his ear and heard a sharp, off-key beeping. Puzzled, he squinted at the phone's backlit digital display.

ALL DONE, it said.

As Mulder glared at it in helpless rage, it went on: BYE-BYE.

"We'll see about that," he vowed, hearing his words fade away into the vast silence of the night.

LES MARTIN has written dozens of books for young readers, including the RAIDERS OF THE LOST ARK and INDIANA JONES AND THE TEMPLE OF DOOM movie storybooks, and many Young Indiana Jones middle-grade novels. He has also adapted many classic works of fiction for young readers, including THE LAST OF THE MOHICANS, EDGAR ALLAN POE'S TALES OF TERROR, and THE VAMPIRE. Mr. Martin is a resident of New York City.